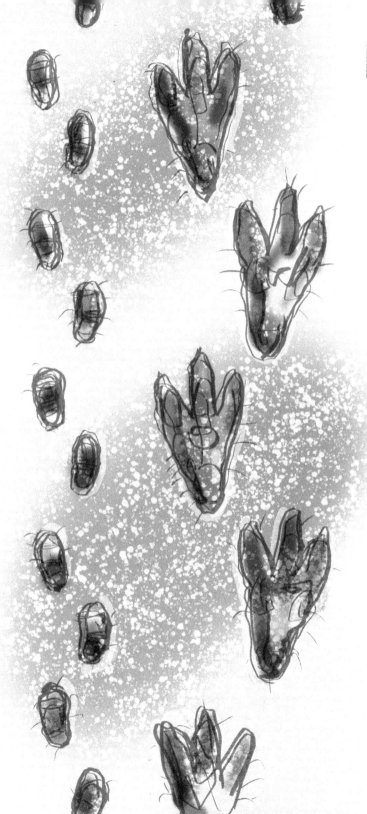

2024 written by Dale Neal and Illustrated by Mark Millicent
Cover design by Cathy Hargreaves at Slim Creative
Dale Neal & Mark Millicent are part of HB Publishing House.

The Dinosaur and Me.
HB Publishing House, 21, NG13 7AW
British Library Catalogue in Publication Data: a catalogue record for this book is available from the British Library.
ISBN: 9781739300425

THe diNOSaUr aND Me

By Dale Neal

ILLUSTRATED By MarK MilliCent

I've never fitted in at school
or had that many friends,
I don't go to the parties
that the cooler kids attend.

whenever we play football,
I'm the last one to be picked,

I broke the kitchen window
with the last ball that I kicked!

BUT I'VE GOT
SOMETHING

MAGICAL

THAT NO ONE IN THE
WORLD
WILL EVER HAVE, MAN
OR WOMAN, LITTLE BOY
OR GIRL...

My best friend is a dinosaur,
(T Rex to be precise),
he lived for sixty million years
inside a block of ice.

The ice thawed out
and all about
our neighborhood he roamed,
looking for a friendly face
or place to call his own.

He took a fall and stubbed his toe
and then I heard him yelp,
So I stroked his paw and broken claw
and asked if I could help?

He asked if he could see his friends
but then when I explained,
that all the dinosaurs were

GONE

and only he remained...

He said, "Oh dear," and shed a tear
- for those he used to know,
in times before the dinosaur,
was frozen in the snow.

I told him,

"I will be your friend,"

and shook the tiny hand,
of the most enormous 'saurus
that has ever roamed this land.

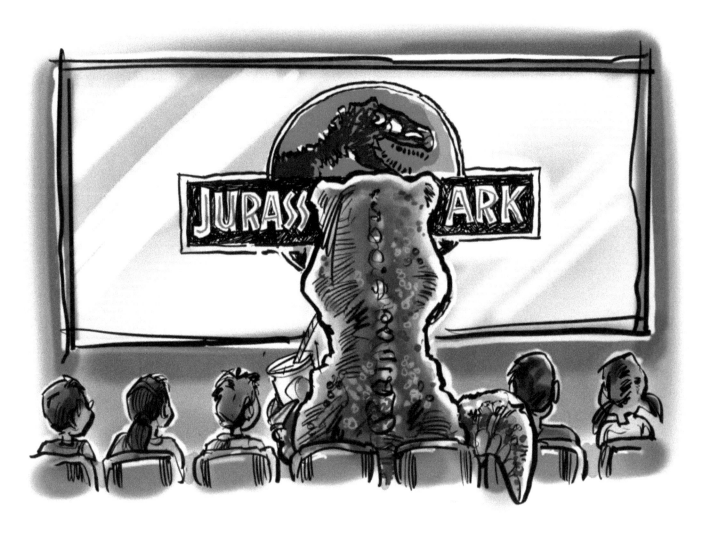

I thought it best, lest people stressed,
we visited somewhere dark.
I took him to the cinema,
to watch 'Jurassic Park'.

We went into a restaurant
to get a bite to eat,
he ate the meat and every sweet
- yet wasn't quite replete.

Steaks and cakes and pasta bakes,
each burger, pie and chop,
he scoffed the lot and when he stopped
he even ate the shop!

Sometimes my dino friend and I
go walking in the park,

where people gawp,
the birds all squawk
and all the dogs go bark!

Then everyone takes photographs
and videos galore,

It seems they've never EVER seen
a real dinosaur before.

when he sees my dinosaur
the poor park warden frowns,
he knows he's prone
to bury bones
a hundred metres down.

I throw a stick and in a tick,
he brings me back a tree,

and I pooper scoop his

super poopers

in a JCB.

So now the other kids in class
all think I'm really cool,
as I'm the only one who rides
a dinosaur to school.

And boys who used to bully me,
don't bug me anymore,
they're terrified that if they tried,
they'd hear my dino' ROAR!

Now every day we laugh and play,
together all the time,
he knows that I'm his best friend
and I know that he is mine.

I used to always feel alone
and so, he says, did he,
but now we're friends until the end
... the dinosaur and me.

Dale Neal writes the funny words

Mark Millicent draws the funny pictures

'Quite a scary dinosaur'
Steven Skeelburk

Blimey, that's a lot of poop!'
Vidal Baboon

Coming Soon

If you loved this book, you should check out what's coming next!

My Weasel has Measels

By Dale Neal & Mark Millicent

Let's be friends...

www.hbpublishinghouse.co.uk

📷 hb_publishing_house

f HB Publishing House

♪ hb_publishing_house

9 781739 300425